MONTVILLE TWP. PUBLIC LIBRARY

Montville, N.J. 07045

ON LINE

S0-AFS-702

MORRIS AUTOMATED INFORMATION NETWORK

0 1021 0068815 3

EJ
Kelle
Keller, Holly

94-19-01

Maxine in the Middle

MONTVILLE TWP. PUBLIC LIBRARY
90 HORSENECK ROAD
MONTVILLE, NJ 07045

Maxine in the Middle

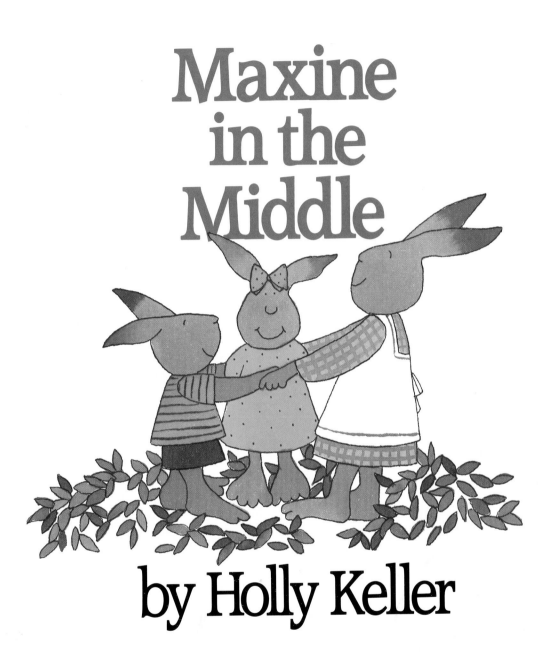

by Holly Keller

Greenwillow Books New York

Watercolor paints and a black pen
were used for the full-color art.
The text type is ITC Cushing Book.

Copyright © 1989 by Holly Keller
All rights reserved. No part of this book
may be reproduced or utilized in any form
or by any means, electronic or mechanical,
including photocopying, recording or by
any information storage and retrieval
system, without permission in writing
from the Publisher, Greenwillow Books,
a division of William Morrow & Company, Inc.,
105 Madison Avenue, New York, N.Y. 10016.
Printed in Singapore by Tien Wah Press
First Edition
10 9 8 7 6 5 4 3 2 1

Library of Congress Cataloging-in-Publication Data

Keller, Holly.
Maxine in the middle / by Holly Keller.
p.   cm.
Summary: Tired of being neither the
oldest nor the youngest child,
Maxine decides to leave home.
ISBN 0-688-08150-9.
ISBN 0-688-08151-7 (lib. bdg.)
[1. Brothers and sisters—Fiction.]
I. Title.   PZ7.K28132Max   1989
[E]—dc19   88-18783   CIP   AC

94
r Ak Sunra
4.98

FOR COREY

IN HER EIGHTEENTH YEAR

Rosalie was the oldest,
Sammy was the baby,
and Maxine was in the middle.

On the first day of school Rosalie had
a new dress. Sammy had new sneakers,
and Maxine wore Rosalie's dress from
last year with the hem taken up.
"It looks pretty on you too, dear,"
Mama said.

Rosalie got new crayons because she
needed them for the second grade.
Sammy and Maxine got a box to share,
but Sammy didn't want to share, so he
hid all the good colors.
"Don't fight with Sammy, Maxine," Mama
scolded when Maxine began to cry.

On Halloween Rosalie wanted to be a gypsy and
Sammy wanted to be a clown. Maxine said she didn't
mind just being a ghost, but she did.

"That's a nice costume, Maxine," Mrs. Bloom said.
"Boo," Maxine grumbled, and she went home to watch TV.

When Mama and Papa went downtown, Rosalie got
to stay with a friend. Sammy and Maxine had to stay
home with a babysitter.
The babysitter read stories to Sammy so he wouldn't
be unhappy, and Maxine had to play by herself.

Christmas was the worst of all.
Rosalie told Maxine that Santa didn't really
come down the chimney. She knew because
last year she stayed up a long time watching
and she didn't see him.
"But don't tell Sammy," she whispered,
"because he'll cry!"

Then at Christmas dinner Rosalie got
the first drumstick because she was
the oldest. Sammy got the other one
because he was the youngest.
"You can have the wishbone, Maxine,"
Mama said, but Maxine didn't want it.

She pushed back her chair and said,
"Goodbye, I'm leaving."

Maxine put on her jacket and went all the way to
the tree house at the edge of the yard, where Mama
could still see her from the kitchen window.

The house was very quiet.

Rosalie put her new ball back under the tree.
"It won't be any fun with just you," she said to Sammy.

Sammy had a set of cards for Old Maid, but he didn't want to play with only Rosalie.

"We'll always know who has her," he said sadly.

"Maybe we should get Maxine back," Rosalie said.

"How?" Sammy asked.

Rosalie closed her eyes to think.

"I know," she said at last. "We'll make a party.
Maxine loves parties."

"With ice cream," Sammy added.

It had started snowing, and Maxine was cold
and hungry.

"You're invited to a party," Rosalie called up to her.

"I can't hear you," Maxine called back.

"We'll have ice cream," Sammy shouted.

"No," Maxine shouted louder.

But in a little while she came down.

Montville Township Public Library   9403066

Rosalie arranged the stools in a circle, and Sammy
put a cherry on Maxine's ice cream.

They had a race around the kitchen table, but nobody knew where it began, so nobody could be first or last.

They played monkey-in-the-middle with Rosalie's
new ball, but Maxine never had to be the monkey.

And Sammy made sure that Maxine
never picked the Old Maid.

Mama served doughnut holes and peanut butter
and jelly without bread for a snack, just to show
Maxine that sometimes middle things are best,
and Maxine giggled.

"Will you stay now?" Sammy asked.

"Maybe," Maxine said.

    And they gave her twenty kisses all her own.

"That was a nice party," Maxine said, and she stretched out in front of the fire for a nap. Rosalie and Sammy were tired too, and Mama covered them all with one big quilt.

MONTVILLE TWP. PUBLIC LIBRARY
Montville, N.J. 07045